Willow the Wild Pony

The ponies galloped over the hillside and out of sight.

"Wait for me!" Willow whinnied.

"You can't go with them," Hannah said softly. "You live with me. You're a tame pony."

"But I don't want to be tame!" Willow neighed.

Jenny Dale's PONY TALES™

Willow the Wild Pony

by Jenny Dale

illustrated by Frank Rodgers

SCHOLASTIC INC.

NEW YORK   TORONTO   LONDON   AUCKLAND   SYDNEY

MEXICO CITY   NEW DELHI   HONG KONG   BUENOS AIRES

ISBN 0-439-79126-X

Text copyright © 2000 by Working Partners Limited
Illustrations copyright © 2000 by Frank Rodgers

12 11 10 9 8 7 6 5 4 3 2 1   6 7 8 9 10 11/0

Printed in the U.S.A.
First printing, February 2006

Chapter One

The autumn breeze lifted Willow's thick mane as she trotted eagerly down the path past her paddock. She pricked up her dark brown ears and pulled at her reins. "This is fun!" she whinnied.

Hannah Grey, Willow's owner, leaned down in the saddle and

happily patted Willow's shoulder. This was the first time that she and Willow had been allowed out on their own. Until now, her mom had always come along, too.

"Now don't go too fast," Mrs. Grey had warned Hannah as she put Willow's saddle on that afternoon. "No quicker than a trot, this first time."

Hannah remembered what her mom had said and eased back on the reins to slow Willow down.

But Willow didn't want to slow down. The plains stretched out in front of them. She wanted to canter and gallop over them.

"Come on, Hannah!" she snorted, tossing her head. "Let's go over there — and let's go faster!"

Hannah wanted to let Willow gallop, but she knew that she shouldn't. "Steady now, girl," she said, tightening the reins.

Willow reluctantly obeyed and slowed to a walk.

Hannah saw that they were reaching the end of the path and pulled lightly on the reins. "We'll be able to go faster and farther one day," she told her pony. "But we'd better turn around now. We've gone far enough for today."

But Willow wasn't listening to Hannah. She tossed her head back. She was sure she could hear hoofbeats — lots of them. What was happening?

"Oh look, Willow!" cried Hannah in delight, as she saw a herd of wild ponies come galloping over the nearest hilltop.

Willow looked up and snorted in astonishment. She had never seen wild ponies before.

The ponies came toward them in a rush of brown and black and gray, manes and tails flying. In the middle of the slope, they slowed and stopped.

The leader of the herd, a handsome brown stallion, leaped onto a rocky mound. He looked down the hillside. Then he threw his head high and gave a wild, powerful whinny that echoed through the air.

Wow! Willow thought. She lifted her head and whinnied back.

The stallion glanced in her direction and then, with a wild toss of his head, jumped down from the rock and took off again.

The other ponies followed. They galloped over the hillside and out of sight.

"Wait for me!" Willow whinnied, without thinking. She leaped forward to follow them.

She had gone only three paces

when she felt Hannah pulling on the metal bit in her mouth.

"No, Willow!" Hannah said.

At the pressure of the bit, Willow stopped.

"You can't go with them," Hannah told her. "You live with me. You're a tame pony."

"But I don't want to be tame!" Willow neighed. She stared at the hillside where the ponies had been. She wanted to be able to gallop like them. She wanted to buck and prance. But Hannah didn't seem to understand.

"Come on," Hannah said, patting her. "Let's go home."

Willow walked reluctantly back along the path to her paddock. Every now and then, she looked

over her shoulder, hoping to
catch another glimpse of the
ponies. But they were gone.

She remembered the way the
stallion's whinny had rung out
across the plain. Just the thought
of it made her tremble again. It
was as if he had been calling to
her. As if he had been saying,
Come with us! Be wild! Be free!

When they got back home,
Hannah led Willow into her
stable. There were two stables at
Devon Farm, one for Willow and
one for Mrs. Grey's big chestnut
horse, Samson.

As Hannah went to get Willow's
dinner, Willow lay down on the
thick, fresh bed of straw and rolled

around. It felt good, and Willow pushed her thoughts of wild ponies to the back of her mind.

Getting to her feet, she started to pull mouthfuls of sweet-smelling hay from her hay net.

Hannah came back with a bucket of pony nuts and bran. "Here we are," she said, emptying the bucket into Willow's bin.

"Yum!" Willow snorted, gobbling up a mouthful of food.

While Willow ate, Hannah's fingers played in the pony's shaggy black mane. Willow had been just six months old when she'd come to live at Devon Farm — a little bay foal with dark eyes, long legs, and a short fluffy tail. Hannah had fallen in

love with Willow right away, and has loved her ever since.

Willow sighed happily. This was her favorite time of day. She forgot about the plains and the wild ponies that she had seen. This was really her idea of happiness — being in her cozy stable with Hannah hugging her. This was where she wanted to be. Just her and Hannah.

Willow finished the last mouthful of food, then turned and nuzzled Hannah on the nose. "That's better!" she snorted.

But a little while later, after Hannah had gone into the farmhouse for supper, Willow found herself thinking again about the wild ponies and wondering what they would be doing now. Galloping? Drinking from fresh streams? Grazing on sweet grass? Willow walked to her stable door and stared out beyond her paddock at the distant plains.

Night came, but still Willow stood there, gazing out.

Chapter Two

The next morning, Hannah came down to feed Willow. It was a school day, and after Willow had finished her breakfast, Hannah led her out to the paddock. "I'll come and see you as soon as I get back from school," she promised, taking off Willow's head collar.

Willow didn't like Hannah
going to school. It had been
much more fun during the
summer when Hannah had been
able to stay with her all day.
"Don't go, Hannah!" she
whinnied, nudging her.

But Hannah went to the gate.
She gave Willow a last pat and

then turned and hurried toward
the house.

Willow watched Hannah leave.
A few minutes later, she heard
the farmhouse door slam and
Mrs. Grey's car start up. With a
sigh, Willow put her head down
and started to graze.

"Yuck!" she snorted. The grass
in her paddock had been long
and delicious in the spring. But
now it was patchy and short.

Willow tried another mouthful,
but it was just as tasteless. She
thought about the miles and
miles of meadow that stretched
out behind the farm and her
tummy rumbled. How wonderful
it would be to graze on that soft,
springy grass!

She thought about the wild ponies. They were so lucky! They could eat whatever they liked *and* they had one another for company. Willow looked around the field. Samson was still in his stable. He sometimes came out with her but even when he did, he wasn't much fun.

Giving a little buck, Willow cantered around the paddock. But it was too small. She stopped by the fence and shook her head. She wanted to gallop. She wanted to race over the hillside, her mane and tail flying in the wind. She didn't want to stay in this small field.

Feeling bored, she started to chew the top of the fence, but the wood pricked her tongue. "Ow!" she whinnied.

She stopped chewing the fence and started to scratch her head and neck against it instead. The rough wood felt good, and she pushed harder against it.

Crack!

Willow reared back in shock. She looked at the fence. The bar that she had been scratching against had splintered and broken. One side was hanging down.

She pushed the broken piece of wood with her nose. It swung on its nail and then, with a creak, fell to the ground. Now there was a gap — just big enough for Willow to squeeze through.

Her heart beat faster. She

stepped over the lower bar of the fence. Suddenly, she was out of her paddock!

"I'm free!" Willow whinnied. "Yippee!" With a delighted toss of her head, she trotted straight down the path that led to the plains.

Soon, Willow felt the springy

meadow grass beneath her hooves. She wanted to meet the herd of wild ponies, but they were nowhere in sight.

With a snort, she started to canter across the plain. "Hello!" she whinnied. "Is anyone there?"

Willow went on and on. The grass grew bare as she went higher up the hillside. She trotted past small bushes and clusters of jagged rocks. Soon, the farmhouse was out of sight.

The sky grew dull and gray, and the wind blew colder. But Willow didn't care. She just wanted to find the herd of wild ponies that she had seen the day before. Where were they?

She stopped and sniffed at the air. Did she smell ponies? She eagerly went forward.

The smell grew stronger. Willow trotted around a rocky mound. There they were!

Willow gave a delighted whinny. This was her chance. Now she was going to be a wild pony!

Chapter Three

Willow cantered up to the
group of young colts and fillies
who were playing on the edge
of the herd. "Hello!" she
neighed.

They jumped in surprise.

"Hello," a black colt whinnied
back. "Who are you?"

"I'm

"I've co

A couple Willow replied.

wild pony."

forward and s onies came

have you come from. "Where

bay filly with a white s ked a

"From Devon Farm," Wi

neighed. She tossed her head proudly. "I broke the fence and escaped."

The black colt looked puzzled. "What's a fence?"

Willow was surprised. "It's a wooden thing. It stops you from leaving your paddock."

The other ponies looked at one another. They obviously didn't know what she was talking about.

Willow gave up trying to explain. "What were you playing?"

...y neighed.

"Tag!" the ...d at her. "Do
The bay fi..."
you want... Willow snorted.
"Yes, ...t off at a canter.
The ...e, then!" she whinnied.
"Cat...
W...ow set off after her and
so...n all the young colts and
fillies joined in. Willow was
having a great time dodging and
turning when suddenly a dapple-
gray mare cantered up with a
commanding whinny.

"It's Storm!" whinnied the bay
filly, stopping in her tracks.

"Tag!" neighed Willow, touching
her with her nose. Suddenly, she
realized that all the wild ponies
had stopped. They were looking
at the mare.

The mare stared at Willow. "I am Storm!" she snorted loudly. "Head mare in the herd. Who are you?"

Willow trotted forward to say hello. "I'm Willow," she neighed. Then she noticed that Storm didn't seem pleased to see her. She stopped. "I'm — I'm from Devon Farm. I want to be a wild pony," she whinnied quietly.

"You cannot stay. Go home!" Storm snorted.

"But I don't want to!" Willow whinnied in surprise.

Storm walked forward. "Go back to your stable," she neighed. "This is not the place for a tame pony like you."

"It is!" Willow whinnied back. She'd been having so much fun with the others. She imagined being able to gallop over the plains with them and graze with them.

"Please let me stay," she begged. "I really want to."

There was a pause. Storm seemed to be thinking about it.

"*Please*," Willow breathed.

Storm looked at her for a long time. "You will do everything a wild pony does? You will eat where we eat? Travel where we travel? Run away from people?" she neighed.

Willow was surprised. Why should she run away from people? But she could tell Storm was waiting for an answer and so she nodded. "I will!"

To her delight, Storm's eyes softened. "You may stay then," she snorted. She walked forward and briefly touched Willow's nose with her own. "I will tell Tor that you have joined our herd."

"Who's Tor?" Willow asked the bay filly as Storm walked away.

"Tor's the stallion," the filly explained. "He's our leader. We have to do what he says."

The black colt trotted over. "Come on! Let's play!"

*   *   *

As soon as Hannah got home from school that day, she raced up the stairs, changed into her riding boots, and hurried out to the stable.

She picked the head collar off its hook and ran out to the

paddock. "Willow!" she called. "I'm home!"

Suddenly, Hannah stopped. The paddock was empty! "Willow!" she gasped.

She raced back to the house. "Mom! Mom, come quick! Willow's gone!" she cried.

Willow had a lovely time traveling across the plain with her new friends. At last, late in the afternoon, they all stopped to eat. The grass on the hillside was short — shorter than the grass in Willow's paddock. It wasn't like the springy grass down near the farm.

Willow went over to Star, the bay filly. "Should we go and find some better grass to eat?" she whinnied. "There's some really nice grass if we go farther down the hillside."

Star looked at her in surprise. "We can't leave the herd," she said. "And we never graze at the bottom of the hill. There are houses nearby."

"So?" Willow snorted.

"So it's dangerous," Star whinnied back. "If we went down there, people might try to catch us."

Willow pawed at the short grass. "But there's hardly anything to eat here."

Star nodded. "We get used to being hungry. It's bad now, but in the spring it will be better."

In the spring? That was months away! Willow's tummy rumbled and she thought about the big hay net and bucket of feed that Hannah would bring her at home.

"When I was a tame pony I used to get big buckets of bran and pony nuts to eat," she told Star. Willow shivered slightly in the cool breeze. "And I had a warm stable with a straw bed."

Storm, who was grazing nearby, overheard and raised her head. "You must forget those things, Willow," she whinnied. "Warm stables, straw beds, and buckets of feed are for tame ponies, not for wild ones like us." She looked Willow in the eyes. "Are you still sure that you want to be wild?"

29

For a moment, Willow thought of Hannah walking into her stable with a bucket of food. She wondered how Hannah had felt when she had arrived at the paddock and found that it was empty.

"Well?" Storm snorted.

"Of course I do!" Willow neighed. But, just for a moment, she wasn't so sure.

Hannah, Mrs. Grey, and Mark, Hannah's six-year-old brother, searched all over the farm for Willow.

"She's not here," Hannah said at last. "Mom, what are we going to do? It's getting dark!"

"Maybe your dad has found

her," Mrs. Grey said. Mr. Grey
had gone out in his Land Rover
to look for Willow.

But when Mr. Grey returned, he
had nothing to report. "There
was no sign of her," he told
Hannah. "I didn't see any ponies
at all."

Tears welled in Hannah's eyes
and she started to cry.

"Hush now, dear," Mr. Grey
said, putting his arm around her.
"I'll look again in the morning."

"But what if we *never* find her?"
Hannah sobbed.

"We will," Mr. Grey said,
hugging her. "We will."

Chapter Four

Willow woke the next morning
feeling stiff and hungry. There
was a cold wind blowing.
Willow's coat was thinner than
the woolly coats of the other
ponies. Hers was not as good at
keeping her warm. She shivered.

A little later, Star woke up and

pranced over. "Do you want to play?" she whinnied. She gave Willow a playful nip and cantered away.

Willow chased after her. Soon, the other young ponies came to join in.

With the sun rising in the sky, Willow almost forgot about being

cold and hungry. "Can't catch me!" she whinnied, galloping off as the other ponies chased after her.

Back at Devon Farm, Hannah woke up and lay in bed, thinking about the horrible dream she'd had. She'd dreamed that Willow had escaped from her paddock.
 Then suddenly, Hannah remembered that it wasn't a dream. It was true. She jumped out of bed and pulled on a sweatshirt. Maybe Willow had come back during the night. Hannah pushed her feet into her slippers and raced downstairs.
 But when she got to the stables, she found Willow's stable empty.

Only Samson was there, looking out quietly over his door.

Willow quickly decided that she was braver than most of her new friends. "Can't catch me!" she teased, as she jumped onto a rock and then scrambled down a steep slope to get away.

The other ponies looked impressed. Soon, Willow was making wild jumps off rocks and leaping over boulders. She could see Storm watching from a distance, too.

Wondering what to do next, Willow noticed a semicircle of trees at the bottom of a steep slope. The way down to them was littered with rocks. "I bet I can canter all the way down to those trees!" she neighed.

Star looked alarmed. "No, Willow, you shouldn't because —"

But Willow didn't listen. "Here I go!" she whinnied.

She set off at a gallop down the hillside. There were rocks to jump over and gravel patches that moved scarily beneath her hooves. But she kept going as fast as she could.

As Willow got closer to the trees, she heard another pony galloping behind her. Soon, the other pony caught up with Willow, then leaped in front of her.

With a whinny of surprise, Willow crashed into the other

pony and was knocked off her
feet. She scrambled up, shaking
her head.

Storm was standing in front of
Willow, blocking the way to the
trees. Her eyes were angry.

"You silly young pony!" she
snorted. "What were you trying
to do?"

"Gallop into the trees," whickered Willow, feeling confused.

"Do you know what's between those trees?" Storm neighed. "Come here!"

Willow stepped forward slowly. After her fall, her legs felt shaky and she didn't like the look in Storm's eyes. She looked inside the semicircle of trees. The ground was soggy and dark.

"Now watch!" Storm snorted. With a front hoof, she flicked a fallen branch onto the soggy ground between the trees.

To Willow's surprise, the stick slowly started to sink. It disappeared with a squelching noise.

Willow started back with a

snort of horror. What had happened to it?

"That is a bog," Storm said. "If you gallop into it, you will get stuck and you will sink."

"Like that branch?" breathed Willow.

"Like the branch," Storm snorted. "Many ponies have died in the bogs on these plains. You must be careful."

Willow backed away from the trees. Feeling very small, she started to walk slowly back up the slope. She glanced up, expecting to see the other colts and fillies watching her and laughing. But to her surprise, they had joined the rest of the herd.

On a ridge high above, Tor was

whinnying loudly. "Men are coming!"

Storm came trotting up to Willow. "Come quick! We must be on the move."

Willow wondered what the mare meant. She trotted after her. As they reached the top of the hill, she saw that Tor was rounding up the herd.

"I must go!" Storm said quickly. "Join the herd. You will need to gallop swiftly now." She cantered away.

Willow hesitated. She was thirsty after all her playing. It wouldn't matter if she had a drink first, would it? And anyway, why did they need to run away from men? Men were nice. Hannah's dad, Mr. Grey, was a man. She trotted away toward a nearby stream.

Tor came galloping up beside her. "What are you doing?" he whinnied angrily. "You must join the herd!"

"I was just going to have a drink first," Willow told him.

To her astonishment, Tor nipped her fiercely. "Do as I say!" His teeth came toward her again. . . .

Chapter Five

With a squeal of fright, Willow leaped in the air and turned to gallop after the herd. They had started cantering now. With Tor on her heels, Willow galloped faster and faster until she caught up with them and dived in among them.

All around her, black, bay, and gray bodies pushed and shoved. Willow could hardly see where she was going. She found herself jumping with the other ponies, racing over stones and down slopes. One of her front hooves landed on the edge of a rabbit hole and she slipped. With a

frightened whinny, Willow stumbled, but found a firm foothold just in time.

Willow was sweating with fear, but with Tor galloping behind her, she didn't dare stop. She galloped on and on.

When Tor finally let the herd rest, Willow was completely exhausted. Her sides were heaving and her coat was streaked with sweat. She stood with her head lowered, breathing in and out in great gasps. There was a wind blowing, and as the sweat dried on her coat she started to shiver.

After awhile, Willow noticed that the other ponies had started to graze. She put her head down, too, but the grass was short and she just couldn't seem to eat enough to get full. No one seemed to want to talk much. Feeling cold, hungry, and lonely, Willow walked off on her own.

As the sun started to set, Willow lay down. She started to think about Devon Farm — the warm straw bed, the sweet-smelling hay. Most of all, she thought about Hannah.

Willow shut her eyes and slept restlessly. It was too cold. She was too hungry, and she was still thinking about Hannah.

As the first gray glimmer of dawn started to creep across the plains, Willow sighed miserably. This wasn't at all how she'd imagined being a wild pony. She raised her head. *I want to go home,* she thought.

Suddenly, she knew that Storm was right. She didn't belong with the wild ponies. She belonged in her stable at Devon Farm. She belonged with Hannah.

Willow got to her feet. She was not going to be wild anymore. She was going to go home. She looked around at the sleeping ponies. Should she tell them?

She took a step toward Storm, but then she remembered how angry Storm had been with her about the bog.

Willow changed her mind. No, she wouldn't tell Storm. She would just quietly slip away.

Turning, she set off down the hillside.

She started to trot, her heart filling with joy as she thought of being home with Hannah again.

As Willow reached the lower slopes of the hill, a damp morning mist rose, swirling up around her.

She kept going — soon she would be home. If she hurried, she might be there before Hannah left for school.

The mist thickened. It was harder to see now.

Willow hesitated. She looked at the ground, remembering Storm's warning about bogs. She could still just about see where she was treading, so she moved carefully.

But the mist grew even thicker,
and the air damper. Soon, Willow
couldn't even see the ground.

She stopped.

The plains were silent in the
mist and she was all alone.

Willow put one hoof forward.
The ground squelched. She
snorted with fear and jumped
back.

She didn't dare go forward. What if there was a bog? She looked around desperately. The white mist was everywhere. Willow wasn't even sure she could find her way back to the wild ponies.

She lifted her head. "Help!" she whinnied. "Someone, please help!"

Chapter Six

Willow heard her whinny die
away. Nothing happened. What
was she going to do now?

Suddenly, through the mist,
there came an answering whinny.

Willow's heart leaped. Someone
had heard her! Who was it? She
whinnied again. "Help me,

please! I'm lost!" She waited for a reply. Would anyone come?

A dapple-gray shape appeared. "Don't worry, Willow," it snorted softly. "I am here."

As the shape came closer, Willow saw it was Storm! She neighed in relief. "How did you know it was me? What are you doing down here?"

"I followed you," Storm whinnied. "I saw you leave." Her wise brown eyes looked at Willow. "Where were you going?"

"Home," Willow answered. She hung her head. "You were right, Storm. I don't belong with the herd. I want to go back to Hannah and Devon Farm."

Willow waited for Storm to yell

at her. But to her surprise, Storm stepped forward and nuzzled her.

Willow looked up. "Aren't you angry with me?"

"No, Willow," Storm snorted. "You are not the first tame pony to try being wild and not like it. Come on. I will show you your way home."

"But what about the mist?" Willow whickered, looking at the white swirling cloud around them. "We can't see. It's too dangerous."

"Not for me," Storm snorted, tossing her head. "I was born on these plains. I have run over them every day of my life and I know every rock and every bog." She breathed warm air gently onto Willow's face. "Follow me and you will be safe."

Willow hesitated. "But what about the herd?" she asked. "What if they move on and you're left behind?"

"They will not leave without me," Storm whinnied proudly. "Tor will wait. Come now."

And so, treading in Storm's hoofprints, Willow followed the gray mare over the plain.

After checking the stable, Hannah slowly walked down to the paddock. It was still empty.

It was misty this morning. She leaned on the paddock gate and stared out at the white-covered plains. It was cold and the air was damp, but Hannah hardly noticed. Tears welled up in her eyes. *"Oh please, Willow,"* she whispered, *"please come home."*

Hannah was just about to go back inside, when out of the white mist two pony shapes appeared. One was dapple-gray — but the other was bay-colored and looked like . . .

"Willow!" Hannah cried.

"Hannah!" Willow neighed back in delight.

The next moment, Willow was cantering up the path to meet her owner. Coming to a halt, she buried her head against Hannah's chest.

"Oh, Willow!" Hannah cried, flinging her arms around her and bursting into tears of joy. "You've come home!"

Willow had never felt so happy. It was wonderful having Hannah hug her again.

Lifting her head, Willow breathed on Hannah's face and nuzzled at her hair.

Hannah started to laugh, even though the tears were still

running down her face. "Oh, Willow! Where have you been?"

Willow snorted, wishing she could explain.

"You must be so hungry and you're all cold and damp," Hannah said. "I'll get you some breakfast and dry you off."

"Breakfast!" Willow whinnied in delight. Then suddenly, she remembered Storm. She looked around.

Storm was still standing at the top of the path. She looked almost ghostly in the mist.

"Come and have some breakfast, Storm!" Willow neighed. "There'll be bran and pony nuts and hay and a warm stable."

At the top of the track, Storm

shook her thick mane proudly.
"Those things are for tame
ponies, Willow," she whinnied
back. "I am wild and free!" She
wheeled around. "Good-bye,
Willow." And with a toss of her
head, she disappeared into
the mist.

"Good-bye!" Willow whinnied
back, staring after her.

"Oh, Willow," Hannah said. "I'm so glad you're home."

Willow turned and happily nuzzled Hannah's face. She knew that there would always be a small part of her that was wild. But here, with Hannah, was just where she wanted to be.